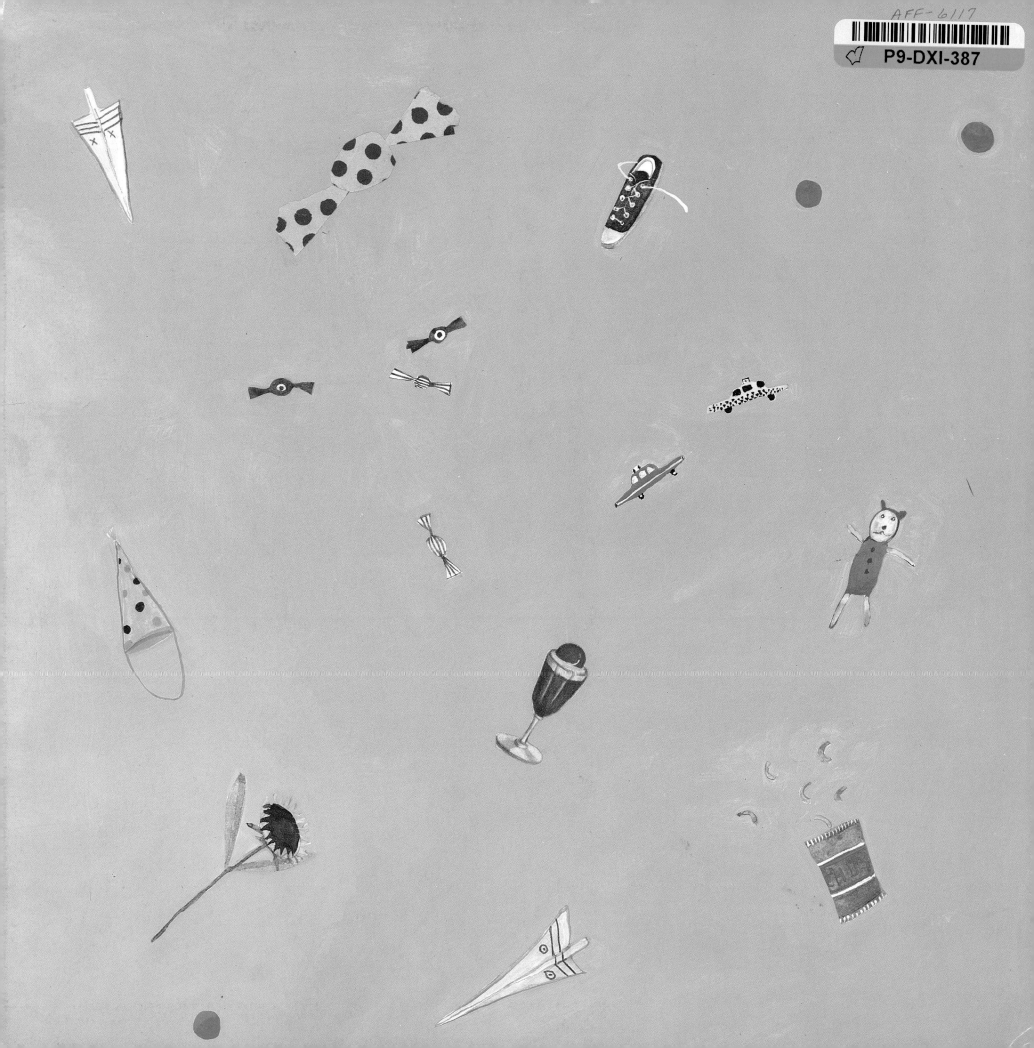

the

BiG

For Kali
—T.M.

For Dino
—S.M.

For Dad, Mom, Chloë, and Kieran
—G.P.

TONI MORRISON

with SLADE MORRISON

BOX

Illustrated by GISELLE POTTER

JUMP AT THE SUN

HYPERION BOOKS FOR CHILDREN
NEW YORK

Text copyright © 1999 Toni Morrison and Slade Morrison   Illustrations © 1999 Giselle Potter

First Edition   1 3 5 7 9 10 8 6 4 2   Printed in Singapore.
Library of Congress Cataloging-in-Publication Data on file.   LC# 98-51948
ISBN 0-7868-0416-5 (trade);   ISBN 0-7868-2364-X (Lib. bdg.)

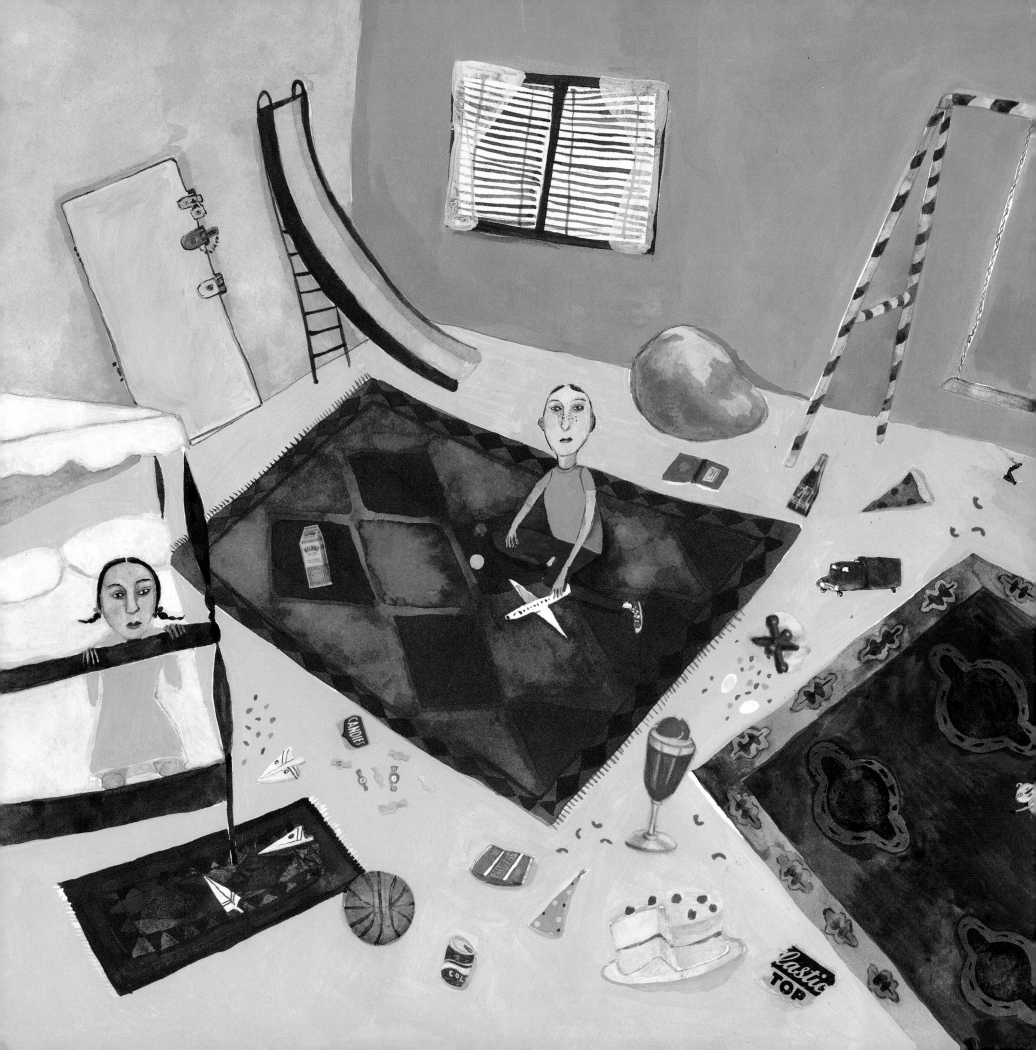

Patty and Mickey and Liza Sue

Live in a big brown box.

It has carpets and curtains and beanbag chairs.

And the door has three big locks.

Oh, it's pretty inside and the windows are wide

With shutters to keep out the day.

They have swings and slides and custom-made beds

And the doors open only one way.

Their parents visit on Wednesday nights
And you should see the stuff they get.
Pizza and Legos and Bubble Yum
And a four-color TV set.
On Christmas day
They got a picture of the sky
And a butterfly under glass
An aquarium thing with plastic fish
Made so it would last.

Oh, the seagulls scream

And rabbits hop

And beavers chew trees when they need 'em.

But Patty and Mickey and Liza Sue—

Those kids can't handle their freedom.

g Hh Ii Jj Kk Ll Mm Nn

Now, Patty used to live with a two-way door

In a little white house quite near us.

But she had too much fun in school all day

And made the grown-ups nervous.

She talked in the library and sang in class

Went four times to the toilet.

She ran through the halls and wouldn't play with dolls

And when we pledged to the flag, she'd spoil it.

So the teachers who loved her had a meeting one day
To try to find a cure.
They thought and talked and thought some more
Till finally they were sure.
"Oh, Patty," they said, "you're an awfully sweet girl
With a lot of potential inside you.

"But you have to know how far to go
So the grown-up world can abide you.
Now, the rules are listed on the walls,
So there's no need to repeat them.
We all agree, your parents and we,
That you just can't handle your freedom."

Patty sat still and, to avoid their eyes,

She lowered her little-girl head.

But she heard their words and she felt their eyes

And this is what she said:

"I fold my socks and I eat my beets

And on Saturday morning I change my sheets.

I lace my shoes and wash my neck.

And under my nails there's not a speck.

Even sparrows scream

And rabbits hop

And beavers chew trees when they need 'em.

I don't mean to be rude: I want to be nice,

But I'd like to hang on to my freedom.

"I know you are smart and I know that you think

You are doing what is best for me.

But if freedom is handled just *your* way

Then it's not my freedom or free."

scream

So they gave little Patty an understanding hug

And put her in a big brown box.

It has carpets and curtains and beanbag chairs

But the door has three big locks.

Oh, it's pretty inside and the windows are wide

With shutters to keep out the day.

She has swings and slides and a canopy bed

But the door only opens one way.

Her parents visit on Wednesday nights

And you should see the stuff she gets:

Barbie and Pepsi and a Princess phone

And a hi-fi stereo set.

On Easter she got brand–new jeans

With Nikes and a Spice Girls shirt,

Marzipan eggs and jelly beans

And a jar of genuine dirt.

Oh, parrots scream

And rabbits hop

And beavers chew trees when they need 'em

But Patty and Mickey and Liza Sue—

Those kids can't handle their freedom.

Now, Mickey used to live on the eighteenth floor

With two elevators to serve us.

But he had too much fun in the streets all day

And made the grown-ups nervous.

He wrote his name on the mailbox lid

And sat on the super's Honda.

He hollered in the hall, and played handball

Right where the sign said not ta.

RULES
1. No Running
2. No Yelling
3. NO animals
4. No Horseplay
5. No Snacks
6. No barefeet
7. No Smoking
8. No Handball
9. No Giggling
10. No Misbehaving
Thank you

So the tenants who loved him had a meeting one day
To try to find a cure.
They thought and talked and thought some more
Till finally they were sure.
"Oh, Mickey," they said, "you're an awfully nice kid
With a wonderful future before you.
But you have to know how far you can go
So the grown-up world can adore you.
Now, the rules are listed on the elevator door
So there's no need to repeat them.
We all agree, your parents and we,
That you just can't handle your freedom."

Mickey sat still and avoided their eyes

By lowering his little-boy head.

But he heard their words and he felt their eyes

And this is what he said:

"But I comb my hair and I don't do drugs

And every day I vacuum the rugs.

I feed the hamster and water the plants

And once a week I hang up my pants.

If owls can scream

And rabbits hop

And beavers chew trees when they need 'em,

Why can't I be a kid like me

Who doesn't have to handle his freedom?

I know you are smart and I know that you think

You're doing what is best for me.

But if freedom is handled just *your* way

Then it's not my freedom or free."

So they gave little Mickey a knowing smile
And put him in the big brown box.
It has carpets and curtains and beanbag chairs
But the door has three big locks.

Oh, it's pretty inside and the windows are wide
With shutters to keep out the day.
He has swings and slides and a double bunk bed
But the door only opens one way.

His parents visit on Wednesday nights

Just after their comedy show

With Blimpies and Frisbees and comic books

And Matchbox cars that go.

For his birthday he got a store-bought cake

And an autographed basketball

And a record that played exactly the sound

Made by a living seagull.

Oh, baby seals scream

And rabbits hop

And beavers chew trees when they need 'em.

But Patty and Mickey and Liza Sue—

Poor kids—can't handle their freedom.

Now, Liza lived in a little farmhouse

Where only the crickets disturbed us.

But she had too much fun in the fields all day

And made the grown-ups nervous.

She let the chickens keep their eggs;

Let the squirrels into the fruit trees.

She took the bit from the horse's mouth

And fed honey to the bees.

So the neighbors who loved her had a meeting one day

To try to find a cure.

They thought and talked and thought some more

Till finally they were sure.

"Oh, Liza," they said, "you're a wonderful child

And we really don't want to remove you.

But you have to know how far to go

If you want grown-ups to approve you.

Now, the rules are clear in everybody's mind

So there's no need to repeat them.

We all agree, your parents and we,

That you simply can't handle your freedom."

Liza sat still and avoided their eyes

By lowering her little-girl head.

But she heard their words and she felt their eyes

And this is what she said:

"But I've worn my braces for three years now

And gave up peanut brittle

And I do my fractions and bottle-feed

The lambs that are too little.

Will the crows not scream

And the rabbits not hop?

Won't the beavers chew trees when they need 'em,

If you shut me up and put me away

'Cause I can't handle my freedom?

I know you are smart and I know that you think

You're doing what is best for me.

But if freedom is handled just *your* way

Then it's not my freedom or free."

So they gave little Liza a pat on the cheek

And put her in the big brown box.

It has carpets and curtain and beanbag chairs

But the door has three big locks.

Oh, it's pretty inside and the windows are wide

With shutters to keep out the day.

She has swings and slides and a water bed

But the door only opens one way.

Her parents visit on Wednesday nights

Right after their bingo game.

They bring popcorn and Chee-tos and pick-up sticks

And dolls that are already named.

For Thanksgiving she had her own stuffed duck

Prepared by a restaurant cook

And a movie camera all set up

With a film of a fresh running brook.

Oh, the porpoises scream

And the rabbits hop

And beavers chew trees when they need 'em

But Patty and Mickey and Liza Sue—

Who says they can't handle their freedom?